# JUST BULL

## ... and a few cow tales

## by Dixie D. Eckhoff

The Old Hundred and One Press
North Platte, NE 69101

Published by
The Old 101 Press
2220 Leota
North Platte, Nebraska 69101
Printed in the United States of America
by
The Covington Group
Kansas City, Missouri
Cover Design and Interior Book Design
by Robin Waters - Graphic Arts Unlimited
Photos courtesy of James J. Griffiths,
Lana J. Lapp and Shellie Griffiths
Edited by Theresa McGahan

Library of Congress number: 2005930227

*Just A Little Bull* by Dixie D. Eckhoff
p. cm

ISBN 0-9721613-2-5

*Dixie's poems and stories are hilarious, sensitive, and moving. She captures the essence and details of life itself and displays it like a beautiful bouquet of images that will make you laugh and bring you back in time.*

— **Weylin Doyle**, friend and Manager of
Maintenance, Bombardier Transportaion,
Los Angeles, CA

*Dixie has given us a witty and insightful glimpse of ranch life in western Nebraska. Her humor shines through as she deals with the tribulations of daily life.*

— **Jack Maddux**, President of
Maddux Cattle Co.,
Wauneta, Nebraska

*I met Dixie by accident. I told her I had a writers' group that met at my house twice a month. She said she liked to write poetry. I asked her what she did with the poems she wrote. She said, "Oh, I just throw them in a drawer and then write another one".*

*She came to our next meeting and brought a few of those poems she had thrown in the drawer and read them. After we had all gotten up off the floor and I had calmed down enough to talk, I said, "You must publish those".*

*Two years later, here is her book. Each poem tells a complete story with nothing left out and in as few words as possible. Two of my favorites are Jake's Secret and The Nodder. I know you will enjoy.*

— **Billie Snyder Thornburg**,
Author and Publisher

As this little volume goes to press, I want to offer special thanks to some special people:

To my husband, Kent, for his interest and enthusiasm, for the time he spent critiquing my poems and stories and working on the cover of my book. I thank him for all the little things he's done to keep me going, including pushing me out the door to go to writer's group meetings when I just wanted to stay home and relax.

To my Dad, Jim Griffiths, for hunting up photos. Sadly, Dad did not live long enough to see the book in print.

To my sister, Lana Lapp, for believing in me, cheering me through the highs, supporting me through the lows, and allowing me to use her and her family as subject matter for many of my poems and stories. She loves me even though she thinks that some of my poems display a "warped sense of humor."

To my friend, Dorothy Havlovitz, who calls me "Kid" and gives me valuable advice about putting both laughter and pain on paper. Dorothy, I love our time together and will always remember what you said about writing from the heart and not holding back.

To LuAnn Wortman, from my hometown, Hayes Center, for her fun illustrations.

To Theresa McGahan for her editing skills and for taking charge of my manuscript and making things happen.

To my cousin, Shellie Griffiths, for helping me come up with a photo for a book cover. It takes a special person to spend a day with me in a pasture sneaking up on cows and bulls with a camera.

Thanks to my sister and brother-in-law, Keith and Lana Lapp, for giving me access to their longhorn cattle.

To my dear friend and publisher, Billie Thornburg, for being my biggest fan. Our chance meeting set me on a wonderful new path at the right time. Without her love and encouragement, these poems would be aging in a box in the basement. Love to you, Billie!

# Dedication

*To my mother, Evelyn Palmer Griffiths, who crossed over on Valentine's Day of 1997. I'm proud of who you were and I thank you for being at my side in my greatest time of need.*

# Just A Little Bull

## HOME ON THE RANGE

## GROWING IN AGE . . . AND WISDOM??

## WHO *ARE* THESE DUDES?

## GONE TO THE DOGS

# HOME ON THE RANGE

# Ivory Clean

When I was just a little girl
of maybe four or five
I said a word one day
that nearly got me skinned alive.
I'd heard that word a time or two
around the neighborhood,
and though I knew not what it meant
I knew it wasn't good.

While playing in the yard one day
I thought I was alone.
I decided I would say it
and hope I wouldn't turn to stone.

My mom was at the window.
She was close enough to hear.
She yelled at me to come inside
and I was sick with fear.

She marched me to the bathroom
and picked up a bar of soap,
ran it back and forth across my tongue.
I felt like I would choke.

If you've never tasted Ivory
I can tell you all first hand
that it isn't very tasty
and it isn't very bland.

Soon I was blowing bubbles
and my eyes were crying tears
and I've never said that word again
in all these many years.

When I listen to some kids today
I think there's little hope.
They should have had my mother
and her bar of Ivory soap.

# Rafter 2 Ranch

We moved to the Rafter 2 Ranch in Hayes County, Nebraska, in February of 1956 from North Platte, Nebraska. My sis, Lana, and I attended Lincoln Elementary School—and later Roosevelt School—while we lived in North Platte. I was eight and Lana was nine. Mom and Dad told us that we would be attending a "country school" where there were eight students.

The ranch was owned by my Mom's uncle, Leigh Fitzgerald, and his wife, Freda. It had been in the Fitzgerald family for years. My grandmother, Grace Palmer, was a Fitzgerald. Leigh was the only son in the family. My dad went into partnership with Uncle Leigh on the ranch.

*Mom outside our "country home" in May of 1961*

It was a new experience for us "town kids". We'd been to the ranch a few times while we were living in North Platte, and I always looked forward to going there—right up until the time Aunt Freda

4

Fitz (known to others as Freda Fitzgerald) started dinner one day after we had arrived. She went outside in full view of my sis and me, grabbed a chicken and wrung its neck. The poor thing was running around in circles without its head. The only thing worse than that was I was expected to eat it. I didn't—although I don't think anyone noticed.

We raised chickens after we moved there, but only laying hens. Cleaning the henhouse was one of my jobs and I didn't mind. It looked nice when I finished and it sure made the hens happy.

Even before we started country school in February of that year, Aunt Freda Fitz gave Lana and me valentine cards from a local boy, Johnny Beard. Johnny's dad, Clifford, was the hired hand at the Rafter 2, and John was a student at Dist. #63. We were a little apprehensive at the prospect of making new friends and going to a new school. Somehow, the valentine cards from Johnny made it all a little easier. It was the first welcome and we felt like we already had a friend at the school.

*Dad and my brother Mark on Sporty.*
*Sporty was a WONDERFUL horse.*

Other students were Ann and Jean Doyle; Roger, Randy, and Ray Floyd; Ron, Kaye, and Johnny Beard. Other siblings would follow in later years—the Karre kids (Doug, Larry, Marlene, and Janet), Mary and Judy Doyle, and our own brothers—Randy and Mark. Betty Miller was the teacher at the time and lived in Hayes Center, thirteen miles away. Betty—known to her students as Mrs. Miller—had to drive within a mile of our home to get back to her home in town, so we rode that far with her after school and walked the last mile from our mailbox.

When it rained, the roads were bad so either Dad or Uncle Leigh would drive us to and from school, which was about three or four miles from our home. We liked it when Uncle Leigh drove us because he loaded Lana and me and the Beard kids in the "dog box" of his pickup. There was a partition in the wooden box atop the pickup bed. We kids would sit on one side of the box, separated from Uncle Leigh's coyote hounds on the other side.

One day as Uncle Leigh was delivering us to school, he spotted a coyote in the Floyd pasture, yelled, "Hang on kids" and off we went. Leigh never passed up a coyote chase, no matter what the circumstances. We were bouncing over the pasture in that dog box, laughing, hanging on for dear life and peeking through the gap of the door to watch the action. When he closed in, he stopped, bailed out of the pickup and opened the door on the dogs' side, releasing the hounds. They gave a good chase, but didn't catch the coyote.

We were late for school. Aunt Freda Tesar was our teacher at the time. We knew as soon as we pulled up to the steps of the schoolhouse door that she was more than a little unhappy. She herded us kids inside, looking very angry. Then she marched right over to the pickup and we knew that Uncle Leigh was in trouble. Aunt Freda (or Mrs. Tesar, as we called her at school) peered over her glasses when she admonished anyone— which was frequently—and now Uncle Leigh was at her mercy. We never knew just what she said to him, but we watched through the windows as she let him have it full blast, shaking her finger at him. Uncle Leigh—who was larger than life—just nodded and mumbled his apologies and no doubt guaranteed that it would not happen again. We all knew, given the same situation, it would.

*Our teacher, Aunt Freda Tesar,
on the steps of our country school.*

In our later years of elementary school, since Mrs. Miller had retired, we no longer had our ride home every day from school, as Aunt Freda Tesar lived in our own community. Dad had a solution. William Garrett had given Dad an old spring

wagon that he had stored in his barn. We girls and
Dad painted it black, and the spoked wheels red.
There were two work horses on the ranch—Pat
and Ted. Pat wouldn't take a step without Ted
beside him, so Ted was elected to pull the buggy.
Lana held the reins and drove us to school when
the weather was nice. Dad had taught us how to
hitch Ted to the wagon and manage the harness.
We picked the Beard kids and the Karre kids up
every day and the seven of us would "buggy" to
school. Ted was staked out near the propane tank
where he ate grass and patiently waited for the
trip home.

*Lana and Randy with Dewey's dinner bell.*

My great aunt and uncle, Ina and Dewey
Wright, lived along the road going to the school.
Every day, Aunt Ina would be at her kitchen window and wave to us as we drove by. Uncle Dewey
was always outside haying the horses by the barn
across the road or standing in front of the house

where he would often ring the big dinner bell and do a little dance for our entertainment. We waved at him and laughed. I don't believe they ever missed a day greeting us.

When the roads were extremely muddy—which they always were when it rained or snowed—Lana drove all of us to school on a tractor, an International 300 that we used for raking hay. Dad made a large, shallow, wooden box and mounted it on the hitch. We lined the box with a large green furniture blanket, with another like it to cover up with for protection from the mud and snow flying off the wheels. Lana was unprotected, though, and on really bad days, she was splattered with mud by the time we arrived. She had to have a change of clothes upon arriving at school.

Our first stop of the morning was at Aunt Freda Fitzgerald's house where we would deliver two quarts of fresh milk in milk bottles. Lana and I milked cows and we always bottled some for Aunt Freda and Uncle Leigh every day. One morning, Aunt Freda came out to get their milk as we drove up. Lana had hit a hard bump and the bottles had broken. I was embarrassed when I held them up. The blanket had soaked up the milk so I didn't know they were broken and empty until I handed them to her.

I guess Lana and I were fully in charge of the milking part of the operation. We did the milking at five in the morning and five at night, separated the milk and cream, carried the skim milk to a small hog pen where we fattened the runt pigs, and of course, delivered milk to my aunt and uncle on our way to school.

# Jake's Secret

Jake had a little secret
he shared only with his wife.
Both he and Dorothy kept it dear . . .
their private way of life.

When evening milking chores were done
and cows at last were fed,
the two of them would slip downstairs
before they went to bed.

They'd push aside the taters,
move the green beans to the rear
of their shelf of home-canned vegetables
to reach their home-brewed beer.

They'd overturn some buckets,
seat themselves and pour their mugs
full of cool, refreshing home-style
stored within their earthen jugs.

Jake would check the new brew nightly,
stretch balloons across the top,
then carefully line the bottles up
and nary spill a drop.

One morn while Jake was chorin'
lifting hay bales from the shed,
his tired old heart just gave away . . .
by noon, poor Jake was dead.

The mourners came from far and near,
cause Jake had friends galore.
They all brought food and blessings;
Dorothy met them at the door.

11

She asked them in to sit a spell
and reminisce awhile.
They shared the pain of losing Jake
and tried to make her smile.

In Dorothy's grief and sorrow
she'd forgot to check the ale.
Balloons were tight as snare drums
and the jugs began to wail.

As the preacher asked for silence
and commenced upon his speech,
a bang was heard beneath the floor,
fast followed by a screech.

Explosions sounded loud and fast,
like buckshot from a gun.
A few good folks just hit the deck
while some began to run.

The preacher grabbed his Bible
as he bolted toward the door
quickly followed by the others . . .
maybe ten or twenty more.

Several ladies cried for mercy,
Elmo Johnson lost his hat.
Gladys Turnbull lost her balance . . .
fell directly on the cat.

They scattered to their autos,
nearly yanking off the doors,
spun their cars in random circles,
with the pedals to the floors.

They were spewing dirt and gravel
as they hit the county road
driving hell-bent for the village
with their stories to be told.

Well, word spread like a whirlwind
through that sleepy little town,
and try—she truly did,
but Dorothy couldn't live it down.

Folks declared that it was Satan
rising up to claim his own.
Poor old Dorothy had to chuckle . . .
Lord! If only they had known!

Now, Dorothy often brews a batch
for mostly old time's sake.
She pours a mug of cool and clear
and drinks a toast to Jake!

# Country School

It was customary in country schools for the older kids to assist the younger ones when our own work was done. We helped them with their reading or mathematics. They were, however, expected to do their own chores.

Our school was more modern than those of earlier days, simply because we had propane heat, electricity, indoor plumbing, and we didn't ride horses to school. Perhaps we did a time or two, but not out of necessity.

*Mark and Pupper*

At the end of the school day, we all had our chores to do. The floor needed swept, window sills dusted, bathrooms cleaned, trash taken out and burned, and chalk board cleaned. The younger kids were never allowed to burn trash but were included in most other chores.

We older kids helped the little ones in winter time with their boots and mittens. At recess, most all of us engaged in a baseball game, croquet, touch football, Annie-Annie-Over, or just played on the swing set. When the weather was cold and miserable, we square danced in the basement of the school house at recess time, as Mrs. Tesar was an avid square dancer. She taught us many of the dance calls. We incorporated square dancing into our Christmas programs, which was a real hit with the audience.

Every year we made invitations for our Christmas program and mailed them out to every family in the community—also to the teacher and families of the Nitsch school, about ten miles away. If you've never been to a country school program I would urge you to see one before they become extinct.

Uncle Jim (teacher's husband) built the stage and the curtains were sheets or blankets from their bed. Our programs consisted of singing, skits, recitations, and, of course, a square dance or two. Most of the folks were attentive largely due to the fact that Mrs. Tesar altered our recitations to include names of folks in the community. Those recitations always got huge applause.

One skit I remember above all others was during the time of popularity of the beatniks in the coffee houses in the cities, playing their bongos and

*Ron Beard doing the beatnik recitation.*

giving dramatic readings meant to inspire or provoke thought. Ron Beard was dressed as a beatnik with dark glasses and a goatee. He played the bongos and recited "'Twas the Night Before Christmas, and all through the pad, not a creature was stirring, not even old dad." He did it so well and folks were laughing so hard they cried. Following the program, cookies and drinks were served in the basement of the schoolhouse.

The community also turned out well for the annual school picnic, held before summer recess. It was potluck, of course. Kids and parents played softball. There were some older couples in our community who had no children in school but were always excited about

*Uncle Leigh at School Picnic*

our activities and never missed a program or picnic. Those that I remember were Dude and Cora Roth, Bruce and Estellyne Doyle, Ted and Babe Fisher, Leigh and Freda Fitzgerald, Dewey and Ina Wright, and Claude and Grace Palmer.

Of course the parents of all the students were sure to be at the programs. They included George and Betty Doyle, Justin and Sally Floyd, Jim and Evelyn Griffiths (my folks), Clifford and Violet Beard, and Bob and Norma Karre. The teachers while we were attending that school were Betty Miller, Shirley Venhaus, then Freda Tesar. Sadly, the school closed in 1969.

Our eighth grade graduations were held in Hayes Center, where we each began high school the following fall. The last little country school in Hayes county to close was ours—District # 63. That marked the end of an era, but I'm happy that I was part of it. I believe that bigger is not always better and the closing of small schools—is one of the great tragedies of our times. A couple years ago I heard a government official say, "Our children are not getting a good education. What we need to do is reduce the size of our schools. We should implement small satellite schools." Gosh. I think that's what we had!

*Schoolmates: Back row: Shirley Venhaus - teacher, Ron Beard, Dixie Griffiths (me), Ann Doyle, Lana Griffiths, and Roger Floyd. Middle row: Johnny Beard, Kaye Beard, Jean Doyle, and Randy Floyd. Front row: Mary Doyle, Randy Griffiths, Doug Karre, Larry Karre and Ray Floyd.*

This is a photo of our "improved" form of transportation when we went to the "town" school in high school. The school bus often stalled on the way to school and all the "big" kids got out to push it. In this 1963 photo, the pushers are Randy Floyd, Kay Beard, Ronnie Beard, Roger Floyd and myself.

# Flying Low

One of the great pleasures of growing up on the Rafter 2 Ranch was going flying with my great uncle in his Bentley B2 two-seater helicopter. He purchased it in 1960 to use for spotting coyotes, checking cattle, and—of course—for fun. The "copter" was a novelty in our area, as in most rural settings. Uncle Leigh enjoyed taking people for rides and most everyone was eager for the experience.

I accompanied him from time to time, but my most memorable flight was when I flew with him one hot Sunday afternoon in September of 1963. It was a typical Indian Summer day. The air was still, the sun was high and hot—the type of day for just sitting around sipping iced tea on the front porch and doing nothing.

We took a spin to the northeastern boundaries of the ranch, dropping low to eyeball the cattle and make sure that they were healthy and that

*Leigh Fitzgerald*

19

there was water in the tanks. Then we veered south to count bulls in the pasture near the lake at Camp Hayes, which was located south of the ranch. We could see that the tanks were full, there was salt and mineral in the feeders, and the bulls were lying in the grass, quite content to sleep away the day. All in all, everything looked good so we circled low and headed north up the Willow Creek towards home.

We flew above the creek on our return flight. As we approached the spillway at the south end of the lake, Uncle Leigh said, "Uh, oh", and broke into a

*Lana enjoys her turn to go flying.*

hearty laugh. I looked down just in time to see a group of frantic, naked, skinny-dipping young men scrambling from the water up onto the creek bank. Bare bottoms were everywhere as they scattered in all directions.

We flew over so quickly that no one was recognizable from that height and speed and—of course—it wasn't their faces that we saw. It didn't escape me that if they had stayed in the water, we would have only seen them from the waist up. They ultimately told on themselves, for at school the next day, several blushing upper classmen approached me and asked, "Were you in that helicopter yesterday?" That was truly the only way I knew who bailed out of the creek—but I didn't tell them that. I just nodded and smiled.

*My first ride. Dad's and my footprints are visible in the fresh snow.*

# Dog Nappin'

Old Jasper couldn't sleep at night—
He used to sleep like logs
'til some neighbors moved in next to him
who had two barking dogs.

They started when their owner
locked them both inside their pen.
Most times it was 'bout midnight...
on occasion nine or ten.

He wasn't sleeping well at night.
His body's old and tired,
and though he had no energy
his brain was really wired.

So Jasper laid upon his bed
with pillows on his ears.
He still could hear them barking
and it brought the man to tears.

He'd spoken to the owner
but it only made him sore.
That fella swore at Jasper
then he quickly slammed the door.

He couldn't call the sheriff
'cause they'd had a little row
'bout when Jasper put a bullet
in the sheriff's wayward cow.

So Jasper laid there thinking
of a way that he might keep
those dogs from yapping all night long
so he could get some sleep.

Jasper's now a happy man,
Z      well rested once again.
He takes a little stroll each night
Z     up to those doggies' pen.

Z

He throws them each a wiener
where in each he's put a pill
that's designed to make them drowsy,
just enough to sleep until   Z

the morning is upon them   Z
and they play 'til twilight sweet—   Z
then comes old, wily Jasper   Z
and he's got a midnight treat!   Z

Z
Z
Z

23

# Chores

Lana and I always had chores to do. I was eight when we moved to the ranch and I could hardly wait to learn how to milk cows. What a mistake! Seems like she and I milked cows forever.

When we mastered the fine art of cow-milking, it became part of our daily routine. Five seemed to be the magic number. We were expected to be up at five A.M. to begin milking chores. We had five cows to milk, but it might as well have been five hundred. Then we milked again at five in the afternoon.

The cows were kept in the pasture south of our house. There was a swamp at the south end of the pasture. Whenever we had someplace to go—like dates for example when we were in high school—the cows instinctively knew this and planted themselves directly in the middle of the swamp. Early on, we rode a black mare named Beauty, who I think was in on the conspiracy. She refused to set one hoof into the swamp. We'd yell, whoop, and holler and those cows just looked at us. I imagined them laughing as if to show us who was boss. They didn't budge. Eventually, we would get them to the corral. There were many times our dates arrived when we were just coming in from the pasture or, worse, milking. Naturally, we still had to separate the milk and feed the hogs.

Maudy was a Jersey, so although she didn't give a lot of milk, it was rich with lots of cream. Maudy was very "contented". Mickey was a Holstein and gave gallons of milk, or so it seemed. I balanced on a T shaped milkstool, put the bucket between my knees, grabbed ahold, and Mickey would turn her head and look at me with those big

eyes, pause with her chewing, then as if to say,
"Oh, it's just you. Well, go right ahead, Dear", she
would turn her head back to the stall and com-
mence with her cud chewing. Mickey never moved
and even on the worst days of milking, she was
quick and easy. What a wonderful cow!

Then there was Wheezey! I'm sure Dad bought
her from Satan. Lana and I fought over who had
to milk Wheezey. We bargained, argued, and
threatened each other. Still, it had to be done.
That cow had to be milked. I remember deals like,
"I'll run the separator for a week if you'll milk
Wheezey". "I'll clean your room, I'll clean house,
I'll feed the pigs for a month if you'll just milk
Wheezey."

*Don Dunn helping me milk Maudy.*

She was a Holstein nightmare who used all
kinds of tricks to avoid being milked. Unlike the
other cows, she required kickers to contain her.
I'd put them on her quickly and tightly. That's
when Wheezey would turn her head, look at me,

and say, "You touch me and I'll nail your butt to the wall". I'd pick up the milk stool and bucket, carefully, quietly sit down beside her, and cautiously reach for her. Wham! She'd kick me. I'd tighten the kickers and begin again and Thunk! She'd have both feet in the bucket. Then she'd maneuver out of the bucket knocking it out of my hands. I'd dump the little bit of milk out for the barn cats, then start again.

Wheezey's trump card was her loose bowels. When all else failed, she'd let loose, holding her tail close to her body so it would become saturated with the remains of the day. Then she'd use it as a whip. Smack! Right in my face. I'd grab her tail, tuck it inside the bend in my left knee, and would turn start once more. Whoosh! She'd whip it right out and smack me in the face again. Then she'd laugh at me—I swear! So, I'd hit her with the milk stool.

This would go on and on until we were finished. Most times, her hooves would end up back in the bucket of milk and it all had to be emptied.

*Our milk cows. Lana is by the barn door and that's Wheezy on the right with her tail up getting ready for me!*

On rare occasions, I managed to get to the house with the produce intact. I believed that Wheezy had a deal going with the barn cats, as they were usually well fed and more often than not, I ended up with an empty bucket to take to the house.

Once in awhile, Dad would show up at the barn while Wheezey and I were going at it and take pity on me. When Dad sat down to milk Wheezey, she became a model cow. I know she was trying to discredit me. Dad was the "big guns" and she didn't mess with him, but gave her milk up gladly, slowly chewing her cud, and smiling while she listened to him tell me what a nice cow she was and that he didn't believe she gave me any trouble. I know he thought I was just trying to get out of milking and I should be nicer to her. Wheezey always won the battles. I wasn't at all unhappy years later when she went to the big milk barn in the sky. I just wish I'd

*Dad and Lana on Roany and Beauty.*

been there to say goodbye and tell her that's what happens when you misbehave.

When I wasn't fighting with Wheezey, I was squirting milk at the kittens. Occasionally, one would jump up onto my knee while I was milking Mickey and happily sit there watching the bucket fill up. On rare occasions one would fall in. I'd fish it out, set it down, and let the other kitties lick it clean. Of course, I had to empty out the pail and tell mom that those cows sure didn't give much milk today.

The cream separator stood in the indoor porch of our home. Lana and I took turns daily turning the crank, then taking the skim milk to a small pen where we kept runt pigs. They were cute when they were small, but it didn't take them long to grow into grunting, dirty faced hogs with a penchant for sticking their dirty snouts on my denim jeans or trying to drink the milk as it was being poured into their pan. The pan was attached to a wire tied to the board fence so they wouldn't root it out into the middle of the pen. Of course, the pan was usually upside down and had to be righted before it could be filled.

Feeding the pigs milk ranked right up there with milking Wheezey. I got very sneaky and circled around behind their little A frame house, trying to be quiet and invisible, but it only took one grunt from one pig and they were on me like bees on honey. Our only consolation was that when they were big enough to go to market, Lana and I had spending money—not much, because we had to split our check with our two little brothers, whose only contribution to the runt hog business was laughing at our futile attempts to outsmart those hogs.

*Lana, Don Dunn and I climbing on the haying cage.*

Lana and I also got in on putting up hay at an early age. I liked haying. It was a real delight, especially compared to milking cows. We had several hay fields and everyone who was available was working at once. Clifford, the ranch hand, did most of the mowing, so he was always ahead of us. Either Lana or I would run the rake. It was a 30 foot rake pulled by an International 300 tractor—no cab, no umbrella, no radio—just hot sun, deer flies, and occasional honey bees. The bees never bothered me until I was in high school and dating. The only time I was ever stung by honeybees was on Saturdays when I had a date that evening. Then I could expect a big bite right on my cheek or nose so I looked like part of Barnum and Bailey's Circus. The bees belonged to Clifford Beard, our hired hand, and he had set hives out alongside the hay fields. He sold a lot of honey, but the bee stings did little for my love life.

Dad bucked hay and Uncle Leigh stacked. We always had to be on the lookout for Uncle Leigh, as he stopped for no one. When we dumped the

rake, we quickly looked right and left to be sure
we wouldn't collide with Uncle Leigh on his way to
the haystack. We had a good team, a good system,
and were able to put up a lot of hay in a hurry.
Sometimes we had two people mowing since Lana
also ran a mower as well as a rake. I always felt a
sense of accomplishment after a day of haying.

*Lana pitching hay*

I do recall one embarrassing day. I was in the
large hayfield a half mile south of the house. It
was circled with tall hills and canyons and the
Willow Creek ran along the east side of the field. It
was secluded, invisible, and inaccessible to anyone who didn't know precisely where it was. I was
there alone, mowing hay. The sun was high and
hot and sweat was dripping off of me. Since no
one was around, I decided to remove some clothing, hoping to catch a little breeze and also to
enhance my suntan. I removed my long-sleeved,
blue work shirt and my blue jeans and used them
for a cushion, doused myself in bug spray, and got

back to work. It was very quiet and so hot that the wildlife were hiding in the trees, not wanting to venture out.

I had worked barely clad for about an hour when I looked up and saw our pickup approaching with two people inside. I shut down the mower, bailed off the side, grabbed my shirt and pants, and hid behind the tractor tire while scrambling to get dressed. I was too late. It was my little brother and the hired hand. The way my brother was laughing, I knew I'd been seen. Clifford had come to relieve me so I could get home and milk cows. By now, my skin was so red that they really couldn't tell how badly I was blushing. I told my brother on the way back to the house that he really could have honked the horn or something. He told me if I didn't want to get caught, I should have kept my clothes on.

*Dixie heading to hay field*

I enjoyed putting up hay—the fresh scent, the big haystacks, and the satisfaction of a good day's work. Recently I saw some haystacks and they brought back memories. Most people in this area bale hay now so I was surprised to see a hayfield with "old fashioned" haystacks. I had forgotten the feeling of climbing a haystack and falling backwards into the soft hay, the hound dogs standing guard, looking off into the distance. They slept there sometimes in the winter, as they could snuggle down inside the hay where the wind wouldn't reach them. The hay made a cozy little nest.

Besides haystacks being good vantage points, we kids used to play "King of the Mountain", scrambling up the haystacks and pushing each other off. I believe the only time anyone got hurt was when my sis, Lana, jumped down a haystack and landed on Dave Dunn, breaking his arm. Aside from that incident, most injuries were only bruises from hard landings due to miscalculations or to hound dogs getting in the way. Hay stuck in our hair and clothing and smiles on our faces . . . ah, the simple life!

*Dad and my brother enjoying our first class swimming pool. When not in use as a tank for the cattle, it was a wonderful place to get cool!*

# Time Alone

The solitude of country life
unlike the city din,
allows for you, reflections
of what you are within.

The quiet of a garden,
the movement of a cloud,
the singing of a meadowlark,
the absence of a crowd.

Time to think of loved ones
and directions in your life,
of special loving gestures
for your husband or your wife.

Time alone for letting go
of things that make you blue,
of deciding what's important
to ensure a better you.

Turn off the television.
Hang up the telephone.
Take one day of your busy life
and spend it all alone.

# Locked In

You won't believe this story
but I swear to God it's true.
It happened to some friends of mine
but I can't tell you who.

He left the house real early.
He was going to a sale.
His wife was staying home that day
to do the chores and bale.

She went into the barn first thing
to look for who knows what.
He saw the open barn door
so he went and latched it shut.

He started up his pickup truck.
It made an awful roar.
He never heard her beating
on the inside of that door!

He drove that pickup down the road,
no thought within his head.
He didn't know he'd locked his wife
alone inside that shed.

She checked out all the windows.
They were high upon the wall.
They were all so very tiny,
she couldn't fit through them at all.

She spent the day in solitude.
She'd kick the wall and cry.
She planned out her divorce decree.
The hours ticked on by.

At last her hubby rolled on in
and went inside the house.
He felt somewhat uneasy
'cause he couldn't find his spouse.

When he heard that woman screaming
he was shaken with alarm
'cause his sweet, hardworking woman
spent nine hours in the barn.

He hurried like a racehorse,
threw the latch and let her out.
The fire in her eyes confirmed
his future was in doubt.

They never said how long it took
to cool that woman down.
But they were laughing like young lovers
when I last saw them in town.

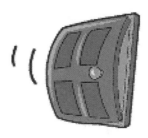

# The Hogs

By now you've guessed that I'm not a hog person. It's not that I don't like them, it's just that I haven't had very pleasant experiences with hogs. I have sneaked quietly up to the hog pen to throw corn out to them, only to be discovered and end up running for my life to the feed wagon. These were not docile hogs. They were raised in the swamp and their large pen housed a pond, so they were hungry, angry, mud covered sows who spent much of their days foraging about in the swamp and dreaming up new ways to scare the bejeezus out of me.

When my children were little, my family and I lived in the house I grew up in on the ranch. Early one spring morning, I looked out the window to see about a dozen sows churning up my lawn. The ground was mellow and they were rooting up everything in their paths. I was in my long chenille bathrobe and I hit the door running—wielding a broom. They were lucky I didn't have a shotgun. I marched those sows west to the barbed wire gate, cleared it with one swoop of my long, pink bathrobe, and followed them all the way to the far end of the corral where my husband, my dad and my brothers were sorting cows. They opened the corral gate and the sows filed through. No one said a word. They could see the fire in my eyes and they knew that it was not the time to speak... They closed the gate, I spun around and stomped back to the house. Pupper, my dad's border collie, followed me as far as the barbed wire gate, laid down under it, and spent the rest of the morning "standing guard". No one ordered him to do so. Even the dog knew when there was trouble.

I have stared a wild boar in the face, his long tusks chomping as though he were about to eat a leg of Dixie for dinner. I have been grunted at, snorted at, attacked by, and run over by an entire herd of twenty or so hogs that looked at the time like two hundred. I have fed little baby piglets with an eyedropper and cared for them until they were thriving, only to see their fat mother lay on them and render my efforts futile. The only hog I like is on my dinner plate with a side of mashed potatoes and gravy!

*Pupper*

# Outhouse Tipping

This story is a true one
that was told to me of late
about a night on Halloween
in nineteen thirty eight.

Some young folks congregated,
piled inside a touring car
and drove out to the Johnson farm
which wasn't very far.

The moon was shining brightly
casting shadows everywhere.
They parked inside a grove of trees
and went on foot from there.

They had come to tip his privy
as they had most every year.
The boys all did the tipping
while the girls were there to cheer.

They saw it from a distance,
made a horizontal line.
They were thirty feet behind it;
they were waiting for their sign.

But nearby in the bushes
old man Johnson laid in wait.
He was watching for the moment
these young folks would meet their fate.

Mr. Johnson was expecting them.
They never failed to show,
so he'd moved his privy forward
just about six feet or so.

There were whispers. There were giggles.
There was no way they could know
that the joke would soon be on them
when their leader hollered, "Go!"

The shadows from the outhouse
surely helped conceal the pit.
Those young men started running
and they fell right into it.

They weren't laughing any longer.
They were such a sorry sight.
The girls drove home; alas,
the men were "walking" home that night.

There was no more privy tipping
on that night of Halloween.
It was nigh onto a week
before they once again felt clean.

Don't know about the next year
cause they never left a trace.
I know they never tipped again
at Mr. Johnson's place!

# The Horse Barn

Ours was one of those wonderful, old, huge horse barns that was a world in itself. I was in awe of it from the first time I saw it and I am in awe of it yet today. I feel so small when I stand inside it and look up. It stands three stories high and was built in the early 1930s under the direction of my great grandfather, Elmer Fitzgerald. At that time, Elmer was buying corn for three cents a bushel. He fed cattle in a large lot north and west of the main house. He also raised horses and mules. During my years on the ranch, it was used only for horses and storing grain.

In the main section of the barn are four grain bins on the west side, two grain bins and a garage on the east. The garage area housed the farm truck, which is what we used to haul the horses when we went to the Maywood Trail Ride. It's rare to see one today, with the old style box, painted red. Everyone uses horse trailers now and they're much more convenient for hauling horses.

The midsection of the barn has a pit where grain can be dumped. High above, accessible by a wall ladder, is a hay mow with a large door and a pulley for lifting hay. Fluffy, a long haired cat, used to have her kittens there every year. There was a large square opening where you could pitch hay from the mow and it would fall all the way to the horse stalls on the lowest level. The lower level consisted of a grain pit, a horse stall on the north side, three and a half stalls on the south side, with a walkway in between. The saddles all hung from ropes on the west end of the stalls. The stalls could house nine horses.

Black Beauty was the first horse Lana and I
had. Dad made us learn to ride bareback before
he would let us use a saddle. Beauty wasn't always
cooperative about being ridden. I'd lead her up
alongside a feed bunk, climb up onto the bunk,
and jump onto her back. She caught on quickly
and would pivot so she was facing me and I
couldn't make the leap. So I changed my strategy. I
put a small pile of grain on the ground and when
Beauty lowered her head to eat, I threw my leg
over her neck. She quickly raised her head and I

*Me on Brownie*

scooted down her neck facing backwards, turned
myself around, and I was mounted. She figured
out that maneuver, too. The day soon came when
she refused to raise her head. She just kept it near
the ground, close to the grain. I looked pretty silly
sitting backwards on her neck patiently waiting
for her to decide to raise her head so I could slide
into position.

As I grew in stature and strength, I learned to
grab a handful of mane and swing myself up onto
her back. She began to expect that and began

stepping sideways. Once again, I changed my strategy. I learned to run up behind her and slap my hands on her rump as I leapt from behind. I was on her back before she knew what happened. I believe I saw a trick rider do that at a rodeo and it looked pretty cool. At any rate, it worked. It wasn't long before Dad decided that we could use a saddle. We were running out of ideas to out-smart Beauty. Dad wasn't always available to saddle her, so he fixed up a pulley in her stall.

Lana and I would hook a rope around the saddle horn and raise it high above our heads, lead Beauty underneath the saddle, then lower it onto her back, and voila! All we had to do was cinch it up and go. We always curried and brushed our horses—before and after riding—without fail. I never trimmed hooves, but I've seen Dad do it enough times that I wouldn't be afraid to give it a try. After we grained the horses, we turned them out of the stalls and they would go bounding out the west gate of the barn. They would then lie down and roll in the dirt, get up, shake off the dust, and head straight for the water tank. We always kept the tank full (it was a large, old, cast iron kettle). We pumped water from an old pump with a long handle—the kind all kids are prone to stick their tongues on when they're covered with frost in the wintertime. (Yes, I did that, too). After watering the horses, we climbed the hill and circled around to the north side of the barn where we kept hay or cane. Lana and I pitched a lot of hay in those years. Haying the horses was one of our many chores—and one of our favorites. Once the horses were watered, they headed up the hill for their ration of hay.

The grain bins of the barn were functional. The grain ran out of small chutes into an old wooden wagon that Dad would park on the lower level of the corral next to the barn. That wagon would be parked in the south hog pen where we would shovel corn out to the hogs—my least favored chore. Sometimes the Dunn boys from Maywood would come to visit Uncle Leigh and Aunt Freda Fitzgerald. We always found our way to the grain bins in the barn, climbed up the steel support rods, and jumped down into the grain. I don't suppose it was the smartest thing to do, but it was fun and the contest was to see who could go the highest in the bin and make the best jump. Oats were itchy, but jumping in the corn was fun.

*The horse barn*

A wooden stairway led to the lower level of the barn. At the bottom of the stairway on the left side was another grain bin. It only held empty five gallon buckets and it was dark. There was never a working light bulb in that room and it always frightened me when I was alone. I was quite brave if there were other people in the barn when I was, or if the horses were there, but I avoided it like the plague if I was by myself.

The barn hasn't been used for many years. It's still standing, but the horses have been replaced with motorcycles, four wheelers, and pickups. How I would love to see it full of horses, hay, and children once again! —not to mention a few chickens scratching around the perimeter. I miss the sights, sounds, and smells of that old barn. Those were good times and I'm so glad Lana and I had the experience of having so many animals in our environment (except for the hogs, of course).

# GROWING IN AGE . . .
# AND
# WISDOM??

# Depantsing
# Freshman Boys

I asked some guys what they recall
of sports and other high school joys.
It seems their favorite pastime
was depantsing all the freshman boys.

Most any day you saw them
driving up and down the village street.
They caught up with some freshmen boys -
then grabbed them by their hands and feet.

They wrestled them inside the car
and drove those kids outside of town
and then amid the screams and yells
they pulled those freshmen's britches down.

They put those boys out on the road
then drove away and left them there.
They had to find their way to town
clad only in their underwear.

They hoped to find some shrubbery,
perhaps a grove of leafy trees.
If they were shy and sensitive
they crawled back on their hands and knees.

They knew where they would find their clothes.
They simply had to reel them down.
Their pants were flying high atop
the flagpole in the heart of town.

The *upper*classmen ruled the roost
and always seemed to have the fun.
The only way to get revenge
was simply by becoming one.

# Dressing Old Chrome Dome

Though my sis, Lana, and I had plenty of outside chores to do, we were no strangers to housework. Mom always found plenty of that for us. She taught us early on how to iron clothes—mostly Dad's blue work shirts. We began with the sleeves, because they would fall out of the way and wouldn't wrinkle when we ironed the rest of the shirt. Next was the collar, then the yoke, the back, and we finished up with the front. Mom was very particular and would have been horrified if Dad had ever left the house in a wrinkled shirt. Those, of course, were the days before permanent press. I guess her training paid off because when I was a freshman in high school, our Home Economics teacher commenced to teach the class how to iron clothes. I was an old pro at it long before then. After giving each of us an item to iron, she raved about my ironing ability and held my example up for all to see.

It turned out to be a dubious honor. She was married to Old Chrome Dome, our Superintendent of schools. The day after praising me to the class, she brought all of her husband's white shirts to school for me to iron! I stood there for an hour that

day ironing Mr. Chrome Dome's shirts while the other girls got to draw up plans for their dream homes.

To this day, I've never got my dream home, but, by golly, I can iron!

# That's a Mighty Pretty Purse You Got There, Cowboy!

Secure in a lifestyle of down to earth upbringing, I spent my time growing up on the Rafter 2 Ranch in northeastern Hayes County, Nebraska. Perhaps I felt a little too secure as I was about to get the surprise of my life one beautiful spring morning in the early 1960s.

My Dad, my sis, Lana, the hired hand, Clifford Beard, and I left on horseback before sunrise to round up cattle from the pasture to bring in for branding. It was still early when we returned to the corral with the herd and the sun was still low in the eastern sky. The neighbors had already arrived when my great uncle, Leigh Fitzgerald, pulled up to the corral in his pickup.

Uncle Leigh was a big man—or maybe he was just larger than life—but I clearly remember his brown felt cowboy hat with sweat stains around the hat band, his blue work shirt that fit tightly across his belly, his levis with the bottoms of the legs frayed where they dragged slightly on the ground, and his pointed toed cowboy boots, dusty with sand and soil of the ranch. He stepped out of the pickup with six or eight coyote hounds following closely at his heels . . . and he was carrying . . . a PURSE! It was white with a gold clasp and double handles and it hung from his hand at his side. All eyes were on him. For a minute no one spoke. We all thought we knew Uncle Leigh pretty well, so this new accessory was a somewhat mysterious addition to his aforementioned attire. My sis, Lana, and I were still mounted on our horses and I leaned close to her and said quietly, "Is that a purse?" "That's a purse," she replied. "What's he doing with a purse?" I asked. "Don't know."

A glance at the fidgety cowboys told me that everyone wanted to ask why he was carrying a purse, but the question went unasked and unanswered. Tension filled the air and everyone was wondering if he had completely flipped out overnight. After a brief exchange of hellos, Uncle Leigh sat his purse on the tailgate of a pickup next to the bottles of vaccine, opened it up, and withdrew a couple of vaccine guns. A few smiles broke out and some jovial ribbing followed. Uncle Leigh explained how he stumbled upon the idea of using one of Aunt Freda's old purses to transport his vaccine guns and how important it is to get the right style of purse for the job. A purse with a zipper wouldn't do as dirt that would accumulate from bouncing around in the pickup would get into the zipper and clog the track. A clutch purse was no good either—not big enough and no handles. A sturdy, roomy purse was ideal, if you could talk your wife out of a good one like that. It seemed like a great idea—old purses to carry vaccine guns. They were functional, kept the dust off the equipment, and you could carry a few doses of vaccine in them. A good idea perhaps, but I wasn't sure if Uncle Leigh's buddies were ready for that.

At the next branding, my dad, Jim Griffiths, showed up toting one of Mom's old purses—a white basket weave with pink, blue, and yellow flowers on it, a gold clasp, double handles, and of course, housing a vaccine gun. One by one, over the course of a year, the neighbors—Bob Karre, Ted Fisher, and Clifford Beard—began carrying purses in their pickups—blue with a silver clasp;

multi-colored star design of yellow, red, and green; pink with butterflies of blue and yellow netting. Occasionally, they would good-naturedly argue about who had the prettiest purse or comment when one of them showed up sporting a new addition to their "ensemble". It may have looked strange to most, especially in our county, but in fact it became very ordinary for the ranchers along the Willow Creek to be seen carrying their purses to the corral.

I don't believe those purses ever saw the light of day in town. Folks just wouldn't understand and might not want to give them the chance to explain the practicality of such a notion. Lana and I giggled at the thought of what those purse designers in New York City would think if they knew their creations were being used by ranchers as vaccine totes at branding time in Nebraska.

# Pockets

A lovely young mother
of three little boys
gingerly moved aside ball,
bats, and toys,
maneuvered her way
to the laundry machines
with arms laden heavy
with half-pint blue jeans.

They were dirty and grimy
with soil of the farm.
The pockets were filled up
with little boy charm,
like fish hooks, steel bolts,
and kernels of corn
and one little pair
had a knee that was torn.

A quick search of pockets
was all that mom did,
then she added detergent
and closed down the lid
and turned her attention
to scrubbing the floor
'til the washer demanded
her service once more.

She opened the cover
and poured in the stuff
that makes laundry smell good
and gives it it's fluff.
As she swished 'round the liquid
so it wouldn't stand
she felt something clinging
and lifted her hand.

She screamed loud enough
for the rafters to shake
as she stared at the limp
little green garter snake.
She busted the door down
and threw it outside
then, shaking, collapsed
on the back porch and cried.

A half hour later
she regained her poise
and smiled as she listed
some rules for her boys.
They'll be heading home soon
and there will be no bad scenes.
From now on, however,
they'll check their own jeans.

# Drag Racing

Drag racing was just part of being a teenager in the 50s and 60s.

Although I had a reputation for driving fast, I never drag raced. I was a passenger on a few occasions, but I was never at the wheel. Well, okay, maybe once. There was a teen dance at the city auditorium in McCook, Nebraska, one Saturday night in the summertime. I was just dying to go, but I didn't have a date. The folks wouldn't let my sis or me drive to McCook. If we didn't have a date, we just couldn't go. As luck would have it, my sis, Lana, and her boyfriend, Keith Lapp, were going and agreed to let me tag along. Keith had a hot car—a green '56 Ford—well known in several counties. In fact, if you ask around today, forty-five years later, I have no doubt that folks will still remember it.

I hadn't driven a stick shift car before, so Keith offered to let me drive. Lana sat in the middle and Keith sat in the front passenger seat. As we passed Perry, an elevator stop near McCook, a car pulled up alongside us with four boys in it. They rolled down the window and yelled, "Hey, wanna drag?" Keith yelled, "Sure!" He quickly traded places with Lana so he was sitting between us. "When I tell you", he instructed, "step on the clutch and I'll shift gears. You steer."

"Okay", I said, and the race was on. Keith and I had great teamwork going. "Now", he would say and I clutched. He shifted. I felt like I was steering a rocket. It seemed like only seconds and we left those poor boys so far behind they surely wondered what happened. We didn't even see them when we pulled into McCook. We turned into Mac's fast food drive-in and they eventually pulled up alongside us. Their jaws dropped and one guy yelled, "Omigod! It's a girl!"

So—I suppose in order to save face—they offered up a proposition to Keith. "Let's race again—this time with you driving."

Keith just grinned and said, "Heck, if a girl can beat you, I can!" They just looked at each other, nodded and pulled away. Now, understand, I'm not advocating drag racing by any means. It's foolish and dangerous—but that night I was a winner and did it ever feel good! Oh, by the way, if you read this, don't tell my kids about it, okay? It's one of those things I never shared.

# The Cowboy

He walked into the dance hall
looking fine as he could be.
His wranglers fit him nicely—
well, as far as I could see.

He had the stride of confidence.
He'd rode a bronc or two,
and now he'd come to town tonight
to have himself a brew.

His heart was newly broken—
it had just begun to heal.
He wasn't ripe for romance,
hell, he couldn't even feel.

He drank his beer down slowly
and surveyed the noisy crowd.
He didn't want to be there.
He was young but he was proud.

He polished off a whiskey
and gave the man his pay.
He tipped his hat and turned
and then the cowboy walked away.

# The Wreck of the Old '57

*(This occurred way back during my college days)*

I only had a drink or two,
or maybe three or four
when I thanked the party hostess
as I stumbled out the door.

I told my sis that I'd be
driving out to spend the night,
though I didn't count on partying
and got a little tight.

My sister lived out on a farm
'bout forty miles or so.
The road was somewhat hard to find...
the sun had long sunk low.

A left turn here, a right turn there,
some thirty miles I came...
no signs to show directions,
and the roads all looked the same.

The tank was reading empty
when I saw a lovely sight.
A dirt road looked familiar
so I turned off to the right.

It seemed to lead to nowhere
and my eyes were getting heavy.
I was speeding down that dirt road
in my '57 Chevy.

An unmarked curve at once turned south,
the car kept going east.
It crossed a ditch and barbed wire fence,
much like a great horned beast.

The Chevy landed on all fours.
Her engine choked and died.
As dirt was swirling 'round the car,
I sadly sat and cried.

The Chevy still had all her parts,
and oh, yes, I did too.
I sat in total silence,
trying to figure what to do.

With hopeful apprehension,
I turned on the starter key
and that Chevy started purring,
just as sweet as she could be.

I gunned across that small ravine
and got back on the road
and continued through the darkness
in a slower, cautious mode.

At last I found the farmstead,
parked the car and went inside.
I had reached my destination
on a wild and wooly ride.

It wasn't long before the sky
was kissed by morning sun
My bro-in-law came to the house
when all his chores were done.

"Did you have some trouble getting here?",
he asked me with a grin.
(Now, how could he have known
about the trouble I'd been in!)

"Not a bit, why do you ask?"
I answered like a liar.
"'Cause your Chevy's parked out front
attached to fifty feet of wire."

So this could be a lesson
if you end up drinking heavy . . .
Instead of driving,
PARK your good old '57 Chevy!

# Cat

Since I got a yellow tabby cat
my life's not been the same.
This cuddly, comfortable feline
has the most unusual name.

I got him from some fellas
who rented me a house.
They swore he was housebroken
and was lethal to a mouse.

They did not misrepresent him.
He is all they said and more.
Each day that cat with the awful name
leaves a carcass at my door.

I praise my babe with animate
and pat his furry head,
then don my gloves and hold my nose
while disposing of the dead.

This cat's a vegetarian -
he will not eat his prey.
He wants his Tender Vittles
served upon a silver tray.

But I love my big old tabby
with the awful sounding name.
Now don't hold me responsible . . .
I'm not the one to blame.

The guys that raised him from a kit
decided as a fluke
that he would have a killer name.
I swear - they called him "Puke".

# Cruiser

It's just a tiny little town—
like many you all know.
I don't think it will ever die,
and neither will it grow.

There's a grocery store on main street;
the coop buys the grain.
The church ladies run a thrift shop
just a half a block off main.

They open up on Saturdays
with coffee and a smile
for those who want to buy
or simply visit for awhile.

But one lovely summer morning
they ran looking for the cop.
They were frightened to the limit
the day Cruiser came to shop.

They hadn't seen this man before—
a stranger to this place.
His hair was halfway down his back,
a beard upon his face.

His lipstick was on crooked,
his mascara much too thick—
and as he moved across the floor,
his high heels went click, click.

The ladies looked him up and down.
Their eyes were full of fright.
His handbag matched his summer dress,
which fit a little tight.

They'd heard of men that dress like this,
but in their eighty years,
they hadn't seen a real one
and it frightened them to tears.

They whispered low among themselves
about what they should do.
They must go get the grocer
and the phone repairman too.

Their businesses were close by
so it wouldn't take them long
to get back to the thrift shop
in case something should go wrong.

Gladys slipped outside
and ran as fast as she could go.
She ran faster than she'd ever run
in thirty years or so.

It wasn't long 'til she returned,
protectors by her side.
Cruiser was still shopping—
no, the ladies hadn't lied.

The men just poured some coffee
and sat down to eat a bite,
mostly just to calm the ladies
and to chase away their fright.

Cruiser was oblivious
to what those ladies thought.
He was terribly excited
'bout the pretty things he bought.

They tallied up a slip and bra,
a dress, and stockings, too.
And Cruiser found a pretty hat
with flowers tinted blue.

Edith rang the charges up,
her hands began to shake.
The men bagged up the purchases—
just for the ladies' sake.

Cruiser took his bag of clothes
and headed toward the door,
The ladies still in shock
regarding what that stranger wore.

They nearly dropped their dentures
and beat up the grocer when
he turned and smiled at Cruiser and said,
"Thank you, come again!"

# WHO ARE
# THESE DUDES?

# The Applicant

"I came out from the city and a job I hope to find.
I sure like the looks of your place, sir,
and if you wouldn't mind
I've prepared a little resume
I'd like for you to read.
It lists my many skills, yes sir!
I'm just the man you need.

"I can do most anything that you require
of a hand.
I can help you with your cows and bulls
and take care of your land.
No, I haven't done this thing before,
but don't you worry none...
I've seen it all on TV and it sure does
look like fun.

"I never rode a horse before, but, Mister,
you're in luck
'cause I'm sure that you could furnish me
a sporty pickup truck.
I'm assuming that the job here entails work
from eight to three—
of course Saturdays and Sundays off—
I must have time for me.

"I'm sure you'll be providing me ten days
of sick leave, too.
A person never knows how often
he might get the flu.
I'll require a vacation, I suppose three weeks
or four—
if Aunt Minerva dies, then I may need
just one week more.

"I can't step in that wet cow poop because
I may fall down.
It isn't safe and there probably ain't
a doctor in your town.
I cannot work with barbed wire—
nothing sharp of any sort—
if I got hurt I'd have to sue your butt in civil court.

"I'm assuming you'll provide a cook
and laundress for my needs.
It is the least that you could do for all
my expertise.
That vacant house just down the road I think
will suit me fine...
and you provide the work clothes
'cause I sure ain't wearing mine.

"Well, yessirree, I think I'm gonna
really like it here.
Oh, by the way, I'm guessing that you'll
furnish all the beer.
So, how about we settle down and talk
about the pay.
If you agree to terms then I could
probably start today."

Well, that rancher took a deep breath
as he looked him up and down.
Then he broke into a laughter as he
gazed upon this clown.
"It's clear, my boy, you never rode
a horse or roped a calf.
Your expertise would only make a
seasoned cowboy laugh.

"There's nothing safe about the daily work
upon the range.
There's things about your attitude
you'd simply have to change.
Barbed wire is essential for the kind
of work we're in.
It keeps those cows from roaming, boy,
it's sorta like a pen.

"It's second nature walking through
that "cow poop" in the yard,
and it's better than to trip on it in winter
when it's hard.
I think there's hazards here, young man,
you're not prepared to take—
in the summertime you might risk
being bitten by a snake.

"We don't have little stiles where you
walk over any fence.
You straddle that old wire and try hard
not to rip your pants.
You'd have to ride a horse here just because
it's what we do—
we have a Chevy pickup, but it sure
as hell ain't new.

"Our time off comes along at times
when all the work is done.
With all we have to do we still know
how to have some fun.
And sick days come when you are sick;
I'll give you all you need,
if I see a bone that's broken, or a wound
that's prone to bleed.

"I need a man to work, my friend
and not just put in time.
The expertise that you possess
to me ain't worth a dime.
The country life still can't be beat,
don't mean to make you frown—
May I suggest you hit the road
and find a job in town."

# Jezebel

The time has come around again . . .
we'll have to run her in the pen.
I'm talking 'bout the cow from hell,
the Hereford we call "Jezebel."

She lifts her head and whips her tail
and paws the dirt and kicks the pail,
looks to her left, then to her right.
It's plain to see she's on the fight.

She isn't docile like the rest.
Each year she puts us to the test.
She's faster than a coyote hound
while chasing us to higher ground.

Don't know why we don't sell that cow.
I never liked her anyhow,
but hubby spoke on her behalf –
"She always raised a real good calf."

# The Night Out

He said he'd take her out to dine
and kissed her on the cheek.
It was the least that he could do;
her birthday was last week.

He donned his newest blue jeans
and shined his boots up nice.
His young wife looked so pretty
and she only changed clothes twice.

They climbed into the pickup
and drove off into the night
o'er the rough and rutted dirt road
'til they saw the city lights.

When they finally reached the restaurant,
the finest in the town,
he jumped out of the pickup truck,
but didn't help her down.

He strode up to the front door
but his wife he couldn't find.
He turned around with searching eyes;
she was 'bout ten steps behind.

He swung the front door open
and quickly stepped inside.
The door slammed shut behind him.
She was on the other side.

She tucked her purse beneath her arm;
with both hands gave a tug
to open up that heavy door,
then stepped in on the rug.

He was heading to a table
in the center of the place
when she walked up close behind him
with a grimace on her face.

He scooted out a chair and said,
"I think this table's ours".
In the center was a candle
and a small bouquet of flowers.

That pretty woman started
to sit down upon that chair
when he plopped himself upon it
and just left her standing there!

The patrons stared in disbelief.
Her face turned shades of red.
Her hubby was oblivious
to what those people said.

She closed her eyes a moment
thinking, "Do I ask too much?"
when a stranger walked up to her
and she felt a gentle touch.

"Allow me, Ma'am," the stranger said,
a smile upon his face.
He was a well-heeled rancher
and of obvious good taste.

He firmly pulled the chair aside
and held it there for her.
She looked into his weathered face
and murmured, "Thank you, sir."

She'd never seen the man before.
To her he wasn't known
but she was positively glowing
like a queen upon her throne.

She bowed her head demurely
to suppress a little smile
while her hubby sat there gaping
like a convict up on trial.

They ate their meal in silence
and in no time he was done.
When he looked across at her plate—
she had barely just begun.

He cleared his throat and took her hand
and said, "I'm sorry, Honey.
My wallet's in my other pants.
I hope you brought some money."

# Skeet

I didn't spend much time around Skeet. He was always out working with the men when I was there visiting. He belonged to my sis and her family, but I know he was very dear to them. So I feel a connection to him also, especially since my sis was so affected by what happened to him.

Skeet was a blue heeler pup when he came to live with the Lapps. They raised him on the ranch and he was a huge part of their daily lives. One day, Skeet began to look ill and wouldn't perk up no matter what Lana did to try to encourage him.

At last she loaded him into the pickup and drove the seventeen miles to the local veterinarian in Hayes Center. After careful examination, the vet suggested that he remain there a few days for treatment and observation.

Lana drove home feeling very depressed and worried about the serious condition of her dog. Skeet spent several days at the vet's and every day Lana called to check on his progress.

"It doesn't look good for him," said the vet. "He's getting worse and I don't think he's going to make it." Tearfully, Lana took a spade from the shop, went to the back yard and dug a grave for her beloved dog. He was full grown, so it took a sizeable effort, but Lana persevered because Skeet deserved a proper burial. She cried and waited for the vet to call with the sad news.

Two days later, the phone rang. Expecting the worst, she was elated when the vet told her,

"He's responding to treatment. The medication is finally working and he's doing well. You can come and get your dog." She made a special trip into town to get Skeet and happily brought him home.

She worried about him seeing the grave in the backyard, as though he would know it was for him. As it turns out, her husband, Keith, was more worried. Neighbors had been asking him what the large hole was for in the backyard. Keith figured it was about his size and said that he'd been sleeping with one eye open ever since Lana dug that hole. I think she let him worry for a couple weeks before she finally filled in the grave.

I don't know if she did that for Keith's peace of mind or for Skeet's.

# The Drowning of Bubba Monroe

The misadventure started
on a lazy summer day
when ranchers, Keith and Lana,
hired a contractor for pay . . .

to move some dirt upon their land
down by a nearby lake.
Now, Bubba hadn't showed yet,
so they thought they'd take a break.

Cousin Dan was there from Iowa;
he likes to come and stay...
he helps with chores around the ranch
and likes to put up hay.

About that time the phone rang.
It was Bubba calling in.
He said, "I need help getting there.
I've overdone the gin.

You meet me at the feedlot.
Bring an extra man or two—
someone to do the driving.
I can tell them what to do."

They headed across the canyons
and at the feedlot did arrive.
Bubba fell out of the semi
looking only half alive.

The CAT was on the trailer,
Bubba's name was on the door.
He said, "Dan, old boy, you ever drove
a truck like this before?"

Dan just smiled and shook his head.
"It's time you learned, my man.
Now climb on up into that cab—
I'll show you if I can."

They drove back without incident
and exited the door,
then Bubba said, "Hey, Dan,
you ever drove a CAT before?"

Dan eyeballed the equipment
sitting on that trailer bed.
He rolled his eyes at Keith
and then he slowly scratched his head.

"I'm leaving now," Keith told them,
"'cause I've got some chores to do,"
and Dan said, "Well, I always did like
trying something new."

So Bubba yelled instructions
as he stumbled round and round
and Dan just concentrated
'til the CAT was on the ground.

Now, Bubba crawled inside the truck
and curled up on the seat—
"I'll move the dirt tomorrow,
cause right now I'm feeling beat".

So, Keith and Dan just headed home.
They'd had a busy day...
the cattle needed sorting
and the horses needed hay.

About an hour later on,
a loud roar made them quake.
There was Bubba on the CAT
and he was halfway in the lake.

Those fellas took off running
just as fast as they could fly.
The CAT had disappeared
and not an inch of it was dry.

They couldn't see poor Bubba—
not a hair upon his head.
It really shook them up
cause they imagined he was dead.

While looking in the water,
they could see the CAT below.
What happened to poor Bubba,
well they really didn't know.

They dragged the lake both high and low
to try to find that man,
but they couldn't find his body
and it sure did bother Dan.

They held a little service
some days later in the church...
A few folks came—mostly those
who'd joined the sheriff's search.

His semi truck was auctioned off;
his daddy kept the cash...
It was all that Bubba had,
there wasn't any kind of stash.

He hadn't any close friends,
yet the local folks were sad
that a young man that good looking
had an ending that was bad.

At the house a few weeks later,
as Keith opened up the door
as big as life stood Bubba.
He was looking pretty sore.

He held a beer in one hand
and he gripped a baseball bat—
"Hey, where'd you park my semi, man,
and I don't see my CAT."

Well, Keith's eyes grew like saucers
as he did a double-take.
He was sure glad Bubba wasn't
at the bottom of his lake.

"Where you been, my boy?", he asked.
"We gave you up for dead."
"Oh, I went to Oklahoma
just to rest and clear my head."

Keith never really knew
how Bubba disappeared that day
but then, he always was a mystery
and never one to stay.

Now, Bubba was plumb happy
that so many people cried
at his "service" that he missed
because he really hadn't died.

# Skunk Trapper

The neighbor's trapping skunks again.
He marks it near a tree.
When I drove by to check last week
he'd tallied twenty-three.

Don't know if he's aware
but he's a hero in these parts
Our attempts at keeping skunks away
result in stops and starts.

They rarely see the daylight
but they congregate most nights.
It's evident they're busy
making little black and whites.

This neighbor is a savior
and he surely has no fear
of trapping smelly critters,
then he hauls them out of here.

We don't know what their fate is
and we're not about to ask,
but we applaud this neighbor
as he carries out his task.

The rest of us just speculate
about where they will roam.
We hope he will release them
at the tax assessor's home.

# The Shooting

One day in late October
good old Bubba felt the need
to stop by Cruiser's house
to drink some beer and smoke some weed.

They both lived in a small town,
reputations widely known.
The beer was purchased locally.
The pot was garden grown.

They sat around for hours
watching TV, getting high.
If the neighborhood suspected,
they'd forget it bye and bye.

The finger pointing started
near the time the booze ran out.
They both commenced to argue
'til it turned into a bout.

Cruiser reached beneath his chair
and blithely drew a gun.
He pointed it at Bubba,
half expecting him to run.

But Bubba was so high
he didn't think he was in peril.
He bolted forth and stuck his finger
right inside that barrel!

Cruiser squeezed the trigger,
then in shock began to fidget,
cause Bubba stood before him
minus one right-handed digit.

They sobered up in disbelief—
there was no time to linger.
They ran around the room
in search of Bubba's index finger.

They searched the room both high and low,
his hand devoid of feeling.
Then Bubba finally spotted it
stuck high in Cruiser's ceiling.

It never made the paper
and they never went to jail.
To this day folks are snickering
about that gruesome tale.

Now, Cruiser never flinched a bit
and Bubba didn't cry,
'course it left them somewhat shaken,
but they never more got high!

# Luv That Chevy!

Farmer threw away a pickup
back in nineteen ninety one.
It had lots of squeaks and rattles
and the engine wouldn't run,

So he towed it to his graveyard
of equipment round the bend
and he parked it by a combine
that would never run again.

Then a relative approached him,
said, "I'd like to buy that truck.
It's exactly what I'm needing.
WOW! I can't believe my luck."

That farmer told the woman,
"You can have that truck for free.
It's just a piece of junk, you know,
it ain't no good to me.

'Cause once upon a time
that truck was sent from up above.
It was red and it was shiny...
'twas an '80 Chevy Luv.

It was good for running errands.
It was handy hauling grain.
It went to school on weekdays
and it travels good in rain."

She dropped a rebuilt engine
in that beat up Chevrolet
and told her family, "touch this truck
there will be hell to pay.

84

I need an ugly pickup
that is mine alone to use—
that no one will drive off in.
I can drive it when I choose.

The dashboard on that pickup truck
was split and faded gray
The brakes were old and nearly shot—
don't need them anyway.

Though dents were few and far between,
the paint was faded bad.
Her family cringed and shook their heads.
They thought that she'd gone mad.

A hole's worn in the floorboard.
The glove box wouldn't close
The handle's busted off the door—
no windshield wiper hose.

She held her head up proudly
and proclaimed, "I think it's nice."
And she didn't even mind
that nest of little baby mice.

That Chevy Luv was hers alone
for all her daily needs.
She drove it on the highway
and she drove it through the weeds.

She drove it through the pasture
and she drove it through the mire
She drove it through a thunderstorm
and to a prairie fire.

She drove it through the canyons
to check the cows and mares.
She drove it to the city
where she drew some highbrow stares.

The box is full of buckets.
Vice grips roll down the glass.
It drinks a lot of Quaker State
and runs on methane gas.

It boasts a hundred thousand.
Sis will never give it up.
And no one ever tries to take
her little pickup truck!

*Lana and her Chevy*

# Alone

*This is a little one I wrote while I was single, before I met and married Kent. Until then, I spent a lot of evenings with David Letterman.*

My telephone's not ringing.
Perhaps it's cause I'm clinging
to the notion that I still look forty-five!!

So I sit here contemplating —
for my white knight I'm still waiting.
Aren't there any men that know that I'm alive??

Yes, I've had some invitations
and a couple altercations...
some were much too young, the others much too old.

A few that asked were married
and one guy last week they buried...
I think my bod's the one that's getting cold.

So, I'm tending to my flowers
just to wile away the hours
and trying not to be a lovesick fool.

Besides, who needs the hassle?
I'm the queen of this here castle,
so why give the crown so someone else can rule!

# Saving Bernie

Bernie had been roping steers
for twenty years or so...
no Super Looper Cooper,
but he gave it his best go.

Matt agreed to partner
at the roping, so he said.
Matt would be the heeler man
while Bernie roped the head.

Their turn was up and they were set,
their steer came out the chute
and Bernie came out swinging,
but it looked like a salute.

Somehow his arm got tangled
up inside his lariat
and Matt knew they had trouble
that he wouldn't soon forget.

The horse went left, the steer went right,
and Bernie was in harm.
That critter pulled him flying
with that lasso round his arm.

Now, H.L. was the flagger.
He was on his trusty bay.
He saw Bernie was in trouble.
He must cut the rope away.

H.L. was on the money
as he pulled his Bowie knife
and he rode straight for old Bernie
just to save that fella's life.

The rope came loose about the time
H.L. could reach the site.
He jumped right down to see
if his friend, Bernie, was alright.

Well, Bernie—he was shaken
but he wasn't hurt at all.
H.L. got up and walked away
and then he took a fall.

He doubled over on the ground
his head down to the dirt.
A roper ran out to his side
afraid that he'd been hurt.

He thought that H.L. stabbed himself—
the folks all saw the knife.
The ropers were all gasping
and they feared for H.L.'s life.

But he was only laughing
like he'd never laughed before,
and the only thing that hurt
was that he laughed 'til he was sore.

He won a little money
and he paid his entry fee,
but he would have paid them double
just to have the memory.

# The Hitchhiker

I saw that fella hitching
out on Highway 83.
He looked to be about my age,
whatever that might be.

He didn't look too scary—
like some hitchers that I've seen.
His appearance bordered decent
his physique was long and lean.

Normally I wouldn't stop
for any highway ranger
but I'd just come from church
and I felt sorry for that stranger.

He is a child of God, you know,
I told myself that day.
If I didn't try to help him,
there would sure be hell to pay.

I stopped my car, he sauntered forth
and opened up the door.
He said "hello", got in,
and put his bag down on the floor.

He asked my destination,
though he didn't volunteer
any information on himself.
I thought it rather queer.

Something seemed familiar
about the face beneath the hair,
and I couldn't shake the feeling
that I knew him from somewhere.

The face had gotten older,
I suppose that mine had too,
but the voice was not forgotten.
It was now my strongest clue.

The realization hit me
when I saw the ring he wore.
He was an old boyfriend
I dumped in nineteen sixty four.

I hoped that he'd forgotten
but that smirk upon his face
was a certain indication
that revenge was taking place.

He asked me to pull over,
then he took my watch and rings.
He lifted all my money
and a couple other things.

He tipped his hat,
then drove my car away like it was free
and left me standing, hitching
out on Highway 83.

# Paris on the Prairie

I pondered as I watched a TV show
called "Simple Life"
Would a Sandhills rancher fare
with Paris Hilton for a wife?

Could Paris cook up dinner
for a hungry haying crew?
Or would she serve up caviar;
perhaps a glass of wine or two?

If you think that girl's domestic,
it's just one of many myths—
To make a simple pie,
she'd have to thaw a Mrs. Smith's.

Could she ride a western saddle horse
or mend a busted wire?
Could she operate equipment
like a washer or a dryer?

And when it's calving season
could she help you pull a calf?
Could she help you sew a prolapse?
That would surely be a laugh.

Could Paris Hilton operate
a chainsaw or a spade?
Would she survive a month
without a butler or a maid?

Well, don't count on it cowboy.
That gal's extremely rich.
You wouldn't catch her pitching hay
or digging you a ditch.

You're better off to look around
and find a gal that's strong
Than to hitch up with a model
who wouldn't last too long.

Now, whether Paris works or not,
nobody really cares
'Cause she looks so darned terrific
in those clothes she almost wears.

# I Get By . . . With a Little Help from My Friends

*Just a Little Bull* began as an exciting, new adventure for me—one I never believed would really happen. Before it finally went to press it had become a project involving my whole family.

My sister, Lana Lapp, Dad, and my cousin, Shellie Griffiths, all joined into the challenge of capturing just the PERFECT picture of a little bull for the front cover. I fell in love with a cute little Microsoft clip-art calf who was licking his nose. Microsoft refused permission for us to use the nose-licker because the use would be for "commercial purposes".

We set out to create our own heart-stopping super star. Lana and her husband, Keith, put out salt blocks and the troops took aim with their cameras. As I headed for home at the end of our "photo shoot", Lana and Shellie each promised to print off their photos and send me the "best" of their handiwork. I waited with great anticipation to see what the mail would bring.

When the pictures arrived, I sorted through a wide variety of bulls—all colors and sizes—some were even licking their noses! One photo did not seem to fit. I decided it must be a group of folks gathered for a branding. They were acting rather strange, however. Each person had their nose in the air and was sticking their tongue out at the cameraperson.

I asked my sis about this photo later. She said they had spent so much time and energy trying to capture a bull calf with his tongue in his nose that Shellie decided they should pose for a back-up photo!

*The Members of the Nose Licking Gang*

Lana and I ventured out once again to photograph little baby bulls. "You'd better watch out," she warned. "That black cow's checking you out pretty good."

"You keep an eye out on her for me," I replied as I inched my way toward her baby. I guess she didn't consider me a threat, though. After all, I was outnumbered by a few hundred to one.

I couldn't help being awed by the incredible beauty around me. I could see for miles. The pastures were lush and green. Multicolored, longhorn cattle dotted the pasture—some gazing curiously at this crazy woman with a camera. The silence was as beautiful as the view. From my vantage point the magnificent horns of these cattle silhouetted against the sky were a sight to behold!

# GONE
# TO THE DOGS

# The Deal

We looked each other up and down...
I kept a wary distance,
but at last agreed to dinner
just because of his persistence.

I grew to like this man a lot.
He was what I'd been missing,
but that hairy beard upon his face
weren't favorable to kissing.

And when I turned my head away
he thought that I was fickle.
I really loved the man a lot.
I couldn't stand the tickle.

He finally asked one starry night
if I'd consent to marry.
I'd wed him in a minute
if he weren't so gol darned hairy!

So, I gave my explanation
and I wasn't very coy
When he told me that *my* hair's so short
I looked more like a boy.

We struck a deal that very night...
I'd grow and dye my hair.
He'd shave his beard completely off
so I could see who's there.

It's just a few years later
and my hair is growing still.
I cover up the gray ones.
I suppose I always will.

And underneath that beard
I see a face that's truly kind,
with a smile I hadn't seen before
'cause it was hard to find.

It's true that married couples
sometimes have to make a trade
and we're both in firm agreement
it's the best deal we have made!

Dixie and Kent

# Nicky

His eyes are black as ebony.
His hair is graying yellow.
A roguish fighter in his day—
He's older now and mellow.

He rarely listens when I speak.
He pays me little mind.
Sometimes when it's late at night,
he's very hard to find.

He's running round the neighborhood
with all his lifelong pals.
He roams around 'til daybreak
sometimes flirting with the gals.

He's lucky I put up with him.
His working days are done.
I'd trade him for another
but he's simply too much fun.

He likes to go for walks with me.
He listens to my woes.
He celebrates my conquests
and understands my lows.

I've decided that I'm stuck with him.
He's too hard to replace.
And it's right to say I'd miss him
and his handsome graying face.

He looks at me as if to say,
"I know you understand".
He walks up close beside me
and gently licks my hand.

# Incredible Moving Objects

Events that happened on our ranch
I know I cannot prove.
It seems that stationary things
incredibly can move!

It happened first to Dad
when he was backing up the truck—
a tree ran up and dented him.
Now, isn't that the luck?

The shed door caused some damage
to the tailgate and rear door.
Don't know how that could happen
cause it wasn't closed before.

When the loader hit the truck cab
Dad was surly as a bear,
cause it never would have hit him
had someone not parked it there.

Now, here's the one I like the best.
I tell it "tongue in cheek"—
that light pole up and moved itself—
"It wasn't there last week."

It's surely not a common thing
but then, my husband, Kent,
said our mailbox jumped a couple feet
and caused a scratch and dent.

Perhaps it's a phenomenon—
a downright mystery
to have attacking mailboxes,
walking poles, and running trees.

But, I'm a true believer now,
of moving things and ghosts—
when I backed up the car last night
I was bashed hard by a post!!!

# De-Skunking Ozzie

I arose one day before the sun.
The sky was clear and dark.
Outside my window by the shed
I heard a mournful bark.

It sounded like our Ozzie—
then the bark became a whine
and I knew he was in trouble—
that sweet old dog of mine.

So I donned my robe and slippers,
took my lantern in my hand
and went to search for Ozzie
on our little patch of land.

I knew just what the problem was
when I opened up the door—
the stench of skunk washed over me—
'bout knocked me to the floor.

I pinched my nose with one hand,
held the lantern with my right.
With gasping breath and teary eyes
I stumbled through the night.

I saw old Ozzie standing there—
his head was hanging low
and how that dog could stand himself—
I guess I'll never know.

His tongue was drooping to his knees.
His eyes were dripping tears.
I've never seen a sadder dog
in all my fifty years.

I called my husband at his work
and told him of our plight.
He said, "Go buy tomato juice.
We'll clean him up tonight".

That sorry dog just gazed at us
with a small pathetic yelp.
He looked to be just begging
for a little bit of help.

We donned our gloves and facial masks
and called our loyal dog.
He slowly made his way to us
enveloped in that fog.

We looked like Dr. Eckhoff
and his faithful ER nurse.
Poor Ozzie was the patient
and he couldn't have looked worse.

His pretty coat of black and white
was now a bloodbath red.
He was coated with tomato juice
from tail up to his head.

We followed up the bathing
with some pretty dog shampoo
and when we both had finished,
Ozzie smelled as good as new.

Now, Oz will chase a skunk again;
his learning curve is slow.
If you know a skunk smell remedy,
please write and let me know.

*Ozzie and Nicky Eckhoff*

# New License Plates

If you live in Nebraska
would you tell me how you rate
our brand new piece of metal
that we call a license plate?

It gave me cause to scratch my head
and wonder what they're thinkin'.
The brightest of the bright perhaps
do not reside in Lincoln.

I studied these new plates at length
to see what was appealing.
It's clear the colors and design
leave most Nebraskans reeling.

I took a little survey—
what Nebraskans cannot stand—
the numbers look as though
they had been stenciled on by hand.

The powers that be in Lincoln
have confirmed my greatest fears.
We'll have these bargain basement plates
for five to seven years!

I'll just refuse to change my plates
of this I have no doubt.
I hope I can rely on friends
to come and bail me out.

# The Nodder

I was reading a Lee Pitts article titled "Accidental Bidders" in the April 10, 2004, Fence Post and was pleased that I didn't find myself among the ten most dangerous bidder descriptions—as I fully  expected. That's because I belong in a different category. I am the auction "Nodder".

I should isolate myself at auctions, for as long as no one is talking to me, I'm a very conservative buyer. On the other hand, if my husband is at my side—as he usually is at auctions—my head begins bobbing up and down. This is my husband Kent's fault! He will make frequent comments to me about a bidder or about the item being sold. I just nod in agreement with him, simply because it saves time and discussion. Usually, though, my eyes are directed at the auctioneer and the activity going on, although my ears are tuned to the man beside me. Suddenly, the auctioneer's helper points directly at me and yells, "YEP". "Don't nod", Kent tells me. "That's an expensive item and you'll end up buying it." Oh, he doesn't know the half of it! The first thing I almost bought by accident was a herd of pigs at the McCook Sale Barn back in 1968. I was going to college there, and one morning after classes I trekked down to the local sale barn. My Dad was selling some hogs that day and, since I didn't get home every weekend, it was a chance to spend time with him.

As soon as I walked into the sale barn I knew our hogs were being sold at that very moment, because the squealing was embarrassingly familiar. Everyone else's hogs were relatively quiet—grunting low grunts. Our hogs had grown up with the run of the swamp as their home and a large area in which to roam at will. They protested enormously at being herded into an indoor arena. "Wild" hogs, one might say, but that's another story for another day.

I slipped onto the bench next to my Dad and said, "Geez, they sound like ours".

"They are", he replied. "Uh, huh, I thought so", I answered, nodding my head. "Yep", barked the auctioneer, pointing at me.

"No, no! She's with me", answered Dad, and the sale resumed amid some polite laughter. I was quite relieved that he didn't have to haul those hogs back home on my account. I didn't go to many sales for a number of years, but have recently taken an interest in attending estate auctions with my husband, who is always on the lookout for antique pieces in need of refurbishing.

"Keep your hands in your pockets and don't nod", he tells me, as I am also prone to gesturing with my hands when I try to make a point. I've come very close to buying old record albums that I can't play, a washtub that I can't use, and Christmas decorations that have seen better days. I have taken to policing myself by standing at the back of the crowd, way back—unless I plan to bid on an item.

Is it working? "Yep!" I have only one purchase of late that I cannot identify or use. Actually, I was waving hello to an old friend—the auctioneer.

# Cold Feet

When January rolls around
he layers up his clothes.
No matter how he's bundled
seems his feet are always froze.

Then February chills him as
he tramples through the snow...
His feet look kind of bluish
and he nearly lost a toe.

Electric blankets haven't helped.
He says his feet are cold—
just one more indication
that this man is getting old.

March isn't any hotter
and I'd help him if I could.
I bought some warmers for his shoes.
They didn't do much good.

Though April brings the springtime,
it's in May the grass turns green.
He's complaining 'bout his tootsies...
sure beats all I've ever seen.

June is busting out all over
blooming columbines and phlox.
I'm barefoot or in sandals
while he's hunting woolen sox.

There's nothing worse than August
at a hundred plus degrees...
He's sweating like a racehorse
woolen socks pulled to his knees.

Now in case I didn't tell you
that the blanket's still in use
and I'm feeling just a little
like a roasted Christmas goose.

September brings a brief respite,
October's cooling down.
By November I'll be digging out
my cozy winter gown.

It's drawing near to Christmas
and we're putting up the tree.
I'm pretty sure you're guessing
what he's going to get from me.

All wrapped and tied with ribbon
it's a one by two foot box.
I bought that frozen man of mine
a year's supply of sox!

# Vacuuming the Dogs

Winter is upon us
and the weather's often cold.
Those two old hairy critters,
well they sure are getting old.

It seems the sun is barely set
when they begin to tire.
They're sneaking in the house at night
and sleeping by the fire.

Ozzie plays with Kent awhile
and Nick lays at my feet
and when it's time for bed,
they both look forward to a treat.

They stretch out on the carpet
and I really do not mind—
the only thing that bothers me is
what they leave behind.

It seems like every morning
I find little strands of hair
that are black and white and yellow
and I know it's from that pair

curled up by the fireplace
or maybe in the hall
and lying right between them
is a chewed up tennis ball.

I get my trusty Hoover,
'cause we really spoil those two
and we favor canine company
as many people do.

So I vacuum dog hair daily,
'cause it's part of my routine
to try to keep this house of ours
a Martha Stewart clean.

One day I asked my hubby Kent
if he would do the chore
of vacuuming the dog hair
so there'd be none on the floor.

He got the vacuum running
and then Ozzie left real quick
'cause Kent had the attachment
and was sucking hair from Nick.

Ozzie had his turn next
and he didn't seem to care.
Maybe he just wanted
to get rid of excess hair.

Now, why didn't I think of that—
it's simple, yes, of course...
If you're going to vacuum dog hair,
go directly to the source!

# Telemarketer

We go to bed at nine p.m.
and try to get some sleep
cause we both arise at five
when the alarm begins to beep.

So imagine my chagrin
when in the middle of the night
the telephone was ringing
and I woke up in a fright.

My husband, Kent, picked up the phone
and listened for awhile.
He said, "Honey, it's for you",
and then rolled over with a smile.

When I get a call that late at night
I always think the worst
and imagine that my family's
with a doctor or a nurse.

But, no, it was a cheery voice
I heard upon the line
saying, "Hi there, Dixie, How are you?
I hope youíre feeling fine".

I answered, "Who is this?"
and then my ire began to grow
when he said, "X Association
and we'd like for you to know—

we appreciate the money
that you sent us in the past
but donations sure don't go far
and the money doesn't last;

so I'm calling you to ask
if we can count on you again.
Would you like to make a pledge
for fifty, twenty, or even ten?"

Well, I'm glad that he appreciates
the money that I gave.
Then I went on to tell him
just how hard it is to save.

My husband broke his leg this year;
I had a heart attack.
My poor old Daddy lives with us
and he's down in the back...

The banker sold our cows last month;
our dog—he up and died.
The coyotes killed my kitty cat,
for days on end I cried.

We had an awful drought this year.
The grass has all turned brown.
We went to see the banker
but he sure enough turned us down.

The power company cut us off,
the neighbors do not speak.
We haven't had a decent meal
in nigh onto a week.

I guess that what I'm saying is
I sure am feeling blue
and I'm thinking that *this* year
we sure could use some help from *you*.

See, times are getting tougher
and we're right next to the edge.
On behalf of your great company,
would you like to make a pledge?

A fifty would be helpful,
even twenty-five, or ten,
a little bit of help
for this predicament we're in.

Then suddenly I heard a click;
the line went quickly dead.
Perhaps that nice young fella
didn't like what I just said.

Kent just laid there laughing
as he listened to me groan
and commiserate upon that man
who called us on the phone.

He likes to stick me with those calls,
he thinks it's lots of fun
to watch me squirm or just hang up
or get them on the run.

He knows that I'll get even,
cause somehow I always do.
Next time *I'll* get the phone
and just say, "Honey, it's for you".

# Old Screen Doors

My husband, Kent, and I ended up at another auction last week. He usually brings home some furniture to refinish and I'm faced with the problem of trying to find a spot for it in our shrinking home. Last week, however, I found a gold mine— not in monetary value, but in nostalgia. I found an old wooden screen door. My face lit up like the Northern Lights! I grabbed Kent by the shirt sleeve and cried, "Look, look". He smiled, and we both stood silently for a minute with dumb grins on our faces recalling memories of our childhoods.

"Boy, you don't see those very often anymore," he said. "I know," I replied. "I guess that's progress, huh?" Maybe to some it is and I know that the old wooden screen doors would look odd and out of place on the modern homes being built today, but give me a big old house with a front porch and wooden screen door anytime.

As the auctioneer rambled on I slipped forty years away in time, remembering the house I grew up in on a ranch in Hayes County, Nebraska. Our old wood framed screen door was on the south side of the house, facing the hills of the cow pasture. It was painted dark green. It was a simple wooden T, with a spring on the side so it would close on it's own. There was a small metal hook that fit perfectly into a round catch that was screwed into the door jamb. You could say that it was our "security system" back in simpler times. It was needed to delay intruders only if the primary alarm, "Tippy", our hound dog, had gone off duty for the night. We never had any intruders but it was good to know that the door was "hooked" by the last one in each night.

When my sister and I were little, Dad carried us through that screen door late at night after returning from the neighbors or from a dance. We were sound asleep in his arms. Years later, we carried buckets of milk through that old screen door onto the porch where the cream separator stood like a stern taskmaster. We carried in groceries from town and clothes fresh off the clothesline for mom, school books, lost kittens, shivering baby calves that had the misfortune to be born in a blizzard, and eventually, flowers from some wonderful, love-struck high school boys.

Since my brothers, sister, and I sometimes hit the door running, the screen would get bulged out and soon be ripped completely. We were told in no uncertain terms not to push on the screen. Dad would soon replace it and it would be good as new. After that happened a couple of times, he nailed a small board across the screen door where our hands would push on the screen. That kept everything intact and pretty much eliminated repairs. For extra measure, he also nailed a foot guard across the bottom for those times when our hands were full and we simply kicked the screen door open. Eventually we would push out the bottom of the screen to the point of creating an entryway for the cats.

"Country charm" best describes how I feel about old wooden screen doors. Just try pushing an aluminum screen door open—immobile and always latched. A whooshing sound from the hydraulic gizmo doesn't have the wonderful twang of an old spring guard. Handles don't just come loose on aluminum doors—they break and must be replaced. A wooden screen door handle, on the other hand, just needs a little tweak with a screwdriver and it's good as new. Fresh air breezes through the entire doorway of the old wooden screen doors instead of just the upper half of the door like those manufactured today.

I was aware of the auctioneer approaching that piece of wood and rusty screen that had just transported me back in time. I looked expectantly at my husband. "I know", he said, "but it won't fit on our patio doors".

"Yes, but maybe we could replace the inside door to the antique room with a nice old wooden screen door".

Minutes later, as he was about to bid on that door, I stopped him. "No, I don't want it. It belongs to someone else. I want mine with my own memories".

I'm going back to the home I grew up in and I'm going to retrieve that wooden screen door. I know it was replaced years ago with an aluminum door, but I'm sure it's stored in the old chicken house or in the haymow of the old milking barn.

Call me nostalgic, but I doubt very much that in another forty years some woman will nudge her husband at an auction and say, "Look, honey, at that lovely old aluminum screen door." I guarantee, it won't happen.

# The Visitor

I heard them talk about you once
when I was just a child.
I flirted with you once or twice
when I was young and wild.

But you paid me no attention.
I dismissed what might have been
and I soon forgot about you
though I knew we'd meet again.

Though many years have come and gone
alas, the time was right.
You journeyed here to see me
on one sultry August night.

You came while I was sleeping
just before the break of day.
You reached your hand to touch me
but I quickly turned away.

I did not want to see you
and your hand I wouldn't hold
although I craved the warmth of it
because I was so cold.

I could feel you linger there,
how long I do not know...
I just ignored you hoping that
you'd simply turn and go.

You seemed to understand, my friend,
I felt you back away.
I promise I'll go with you soon...
for now, I'd like to stay.

And when you come again for me
I'll take my final breath.
I'll smile and take your hand and look
into the face of death.

*(I survived a major heart attack in
August of 2001. This is a poem
that I wrote about that experience.)*

# Too Many Pills

I sorted out my pills today
and put them in a row.
You'd think I was a hundred plus
and feeling mighty low.

I guess between my man and I
the drug store stays afloat.
They roll the carpet out for us
and fill our shopping tote.

There's pills to treat our stomachs
and our achey muscles, too,
some oddball combination
so we don't come down with flu.

A little pill to help my heart
and slow cholesterol
and keep that blood a pumping
so my ticker doesn't stall.

And one to lower pressure,
we both take that I guess
cause when you work where we do
there can be a lot of stress.

A little pill for sinus
and a larger pill for age,
a giant one to temper
all that work related rage.

We pay for those prescriptions
but we've only just begun
cause the dogs are getting old now
but they're not exactly done.

Nicky has arthritis
and can hardly get around.
The pills aren't working anymore—
we help him up and down.

Oz was having seizures.
That was quite a scary fright.
He's taking pills to stop them and
the cost is out of sight.

We pondered just the other night
and wondered how we can
get those hairy critters
on our health prescription plan.

It may not be too difficult.
It shouldn't be too hard...
cause last week some fool company
mailed Nick a credit card!

# The Cemetery

I agreed to tag along with sis
though I was somewhat wary.
She was on her monthly visit
to the local cemetery.

She's the one who keeps the records.
She's the one who sells the plots,
and now she's got my stomach tied up
in a thousand knots.

I figured out she's making sure
that everyone's in place,
and each resident is happy
in his designated space.

It is indeed a quiet spot,
so tranquil and appealing.
Prairie grass provides the blanket
and the stars provide the ceiling.

I suppose I will move in one day.
To this I am resigned.
So I gave her my instructions
where I want to be assigned.

I suppose I'll need a headstone
and a little sprig of flowers.
A crossword puzzle would be nice
to wile away the hours.

I'd like to have a shade tree
cause that summer sun can blister
and I'll patiently await
the monthly visit from my sister.

# NEBRASKA & NATIONAL AWARD WINNER

Early in 2005, Dixie responded to a newspaper announcement that the Nebraska Mothers Association was seeking entries for their literary contest. Dixie submitted her poem, *The Best Bouquet,* for consideration.

In March, 2005, Dixie received word from the Nebraska Association that her poem had been awarded first place in their contest and would be entered in the national contest. Since that time, Dixie's poem also received the first place award in the National Mothers Association contest. The Nebraska certificate is pictured below.

Dixie says of her success, "I think every mother has had the experience of being presented with a "special" bouquet by a delighted child. It was probably easy for everyone to connect with my poem."

# The Best Bouquet
*(The National Award Winner)*

The best ones that I ever got
were never in a flower pot
nor pinned upon the gown I wore
to high school prom in sixty-four.

I do recall the flowers, still,
that I received when I was ill...
roses and carnations sweet,
white daisies were a favorite treat.

Those flowers have become a blur.
They never quite gave me the stir
like those that left me most beguiled
clutched in the hands of my own child.

Dandelions by the score,
growing wild by my back door.
My heart set sail when you-know-who
said, "Mom, I picked these just for you."

# The Book

In my hands I hold a book
that conquers all my pain and fears
It quells my grief and sorrows
and dries away my tears.

In my hands I hold a book
a loving present from my mother.
It leads me through uncertainty
and darkness like no other.

In my hands I hold a book
that's full of miracles, you see.
It says my Lord and she are waiting
on the other side for me.

In my hands I hold the Book—
the most timeless gift of all—
News about my Lord and Savior.
Mom, Look! In my hands I hold The Book.

# Just a Little Bull

## by Dixie Griffiths Stinson Eckhoff

A resident of rural North Platte, Dixie Griffiths Eckhoff grew up along the Willow Creek on the Rafter 2 Ranch, located in northeastern Hayes County, Nebraska. She attended a country school near her home during her elementary years and wrote her first poem on an outhouse wall at the age of eight.

"I wrote poems for years but always threw them in a drawer and forgot about them. A couple of years ago, I took a day off work to attend a book signing by Billie Snyder Thornburg. I felt an instant kinship with Billie. It was her praise and prodding that gave me the courage to share my poems and stories with others. I have also received loads of encouragement from my dear friend, Dorothy Havlovitz; my husband Kent; and my sister Lana Lapp. Kent and Lana both have the dubious honor of being my subject matter in many of my poems and stories. Even the dogs aren't safe." Dixie's poems have been printed in a number of publications including the *North Platte Telegraph, The North Platte Bulletin, The Fence Post*, and *Reminisce Magazine*. Her poem, *The Best Bouquet*, won the Nebraska and the National Mothers' Association awards in 2005.

Dixie would be delighted to hear from her readers. To contact Dixie or order copies of Just a Little Bull: Dixie D. Eckhoff, kedx0622@kdsi.net. Books are also available at many book stores and through The Old 101 Press.

## From THE OLD 101 PRESS:

*"They say you can't take it with you, but you can. When you die all the stories in your head go, too."*

Billie Thornburg, founder of The Old Hundred And One Press, and author of *Bertie and Me, Bertie and Me and Miles Too*, and *Sandhills Kid In The City*, is dedicated to encouraging people to write the stories of their lives. At age ninety, Billie wrote her first book and started The Old Hundred And One Press to publish history as told by those who've lived it.

Write your memories and send them to Billie for review. She would love to do what she can to help you go to the "next step" with your writing. At age ninety-two, Billie is working on her own fourth book, *City and Prairie Bones*, a compilation of stories from an earlier era in the history of North Platte and the surrounding area.

Readers can reach Billie at:

The Old Hundred and One Press
2220 Leota Avenue
North Platte, NE 69101

www.theold101press.com
Phone: (308) 532-1748

# NOW AVAILABLE

### Bertie and Me...kids on a ranch
*by Billie Lee Snyder-Thornburg*
Billie Snyder Thornburg's first book. A humorous and historical account of two little girls growing up on a Nebraska Sandhills ranch in the early 1900's.

**ISBN:** 0-9721613-0-9
**Pages:** 160
**Publish Date:** October 1, 2002
**Publisher:** The Old 101 Press Publishing – For All Ages
**Price:** Only $18.95 - Paperback

---

### Bertie and Me and Miles Too
*by Billie Lee Snyder-Thornburg*
Billie Snyder Thornburg continues telling of early Sandhills life with stories of her brother, Miles, home remedies, Model T's. privies, and old time roundups.

**ISBN:** 0-9721613-3-3
**Pages:** 144
**Publish Date:** December 1, 2003
**Publisher:** The Old 101 Press Publishing – For All Ages
**Price:** Only $16.95 - Paperback

---

### Sandhills Kid in the City
*by Billie Lee Snyder Thornburg*
Ride along with "...Bertie and me who were still trying to find our places in the big world around us" as they move from their beloved Sandhills ranch to Oregon to attend high school. Rich, exciting adventures!

**ISBN:** 0-9721613-7-6
**Pages:** 144
**Publish Date:** June 1, 2004
**Publisher:** The Old Hundred and One Press – For All Ages
**Price:** Only $16.95 - Paperback

---

### If Morning Never Comes
*by Bill VandenBush*
The powerful story of a soldier's near-death experience in Vietnam. "A priceless gift to anyone in search of their own spiritual path...enormously inspirational" - Nora Fitzgerald

**ISBN:** 0-9721613-4-1
**Pages:** 232
**Publish Date:** December 1, 2003
**Publisher:** The Old 101 Press Publishing – For All Ages
**Price:** Only $14.95 - Paperback

### Miracle of the Ozarks
*by Chester Funkhouser*
The touching story of a grandfather's love, a child's belief in miracles, and survival of the human heart in the face of cancer, war wounds, and loss. The reader will fall in love with the beauty and spirit of the Ozarks.

**ISBN:** 0-9721613-8-4
**Pages:** 160
**Publish Date:** 2004
**Publisher:** The Old Hundred and One Press – For All Ages
**Price:** Only $14.95 - Paperback

---

### Are We There Yet?
*by Lori Clinch*
A hilarious look at one woman's experiences raising four sons. Not meant as a parenting guide, but definitely encouraging to parents who need to know someone else has kids like theirs.

**ISBN:** 0-9721613-9-2
**Pages:** 300
**Publish Date:** May 1, 2004
**Publisher:** The Old Hundred and One Press – For All Ages
**Price:** Only $15.95 - Paperback

---

### Listen With The Heart
### Everyday Lives Lived in the Extraordinary
*By Barbara Ann Dush*
Heroes are all around us if we learn to Listen With The Heart. The daily headlines scream bad news, crime, hardship, and suffering. However, behind many of those headline stories are people whose lives speak gently to us of courage, strength, and compassion if we only learn to Listen With the Heart.

**ISBN:** 0-9721613-1-7
**Pages:** 160
**Publish Date:** March 12, 2005
**Publisher:** The Old Hundred and One Press – For All Ages
**Price:** Only $15.95 - Paperback

---

### COMING SOON FROM
### The Old Hundred And One Press:

### City & Prairie Bones
*by Billie Snyder Thornburg*
Billie Snyder Thornburg'sfourth book takes a look at life in the vicinity of North Platte, Nebraska. Billie focuses, especially on the period during which North Platte came to be known as "Little Chicago".

# ORDER FORM

Please send me _____ copies of Bertie and Me @ $18.95

Please send me _____ copies of Bertie and Me and Miles Too @ $16.95

Please send me _____ copies of Sandhills Kid in the City @ $16.95

Please send me _____ copies of If Morning Never Comes @ $14.95

Please send me _____ copies of Are We There Yet? @ $15.95

Please send me _____ copies of Miracle of the Ozarks @ $14.95

Please send me _____ copies of Listen With The Heart @ $15.95

Please send me _____ copies of Just A Little Bull @ $15.95


TOTAL COST OF BOOKS:                        $ _____

NEBRASKA RESIDENTS 7% TAX:                  $ _____

Add $2.00 for Shipping and Handling:        $ _____2.00_____

TOTAL ENCLOSED:                             $ _____


Name: _____

Address: _____

City, State, Zip _____

Visit our Website: www.theold101press.com

Telephone Orders: (308) 532-1748

E-Mail Orders: billielee@inebraska.com

Postal Orders:   The Old Hundred and One Press
                 2220 Leota
                 North Platte, NE 69101

THE END